Who Ate the Last Churro?

Tales and Treats from the Luera Family

by David R. Luera

Prologue

Welcome once again, dear readers, to another mischievous tale from the Luera family archives! I'm your host, David R. Luera, and today I bring you a story that's sprinkled with sugar, spiced with a dash of mystery, and served hot and fresh from the oven. "Who Ate the Last Churro?" is not just a story about missing treats; it's a celebration of family, fun, and the unexpected moments that bring us together. So, gather around, make yourself comfortable, and let's unravel another delightful family mystery that proves even the sneakiest of snack thieves can't outwit the bond of family.

Preface

Churros—those delightful, sugary sticks of joy—are the centerpiece of our tale today. In the Luera family, food is much more than sustenance; it's a reason to gather, to celebrate, and sometimes, to investigate. As we venture into the heart of Granita's 55th birthday bash, remember that every family has its secrets, its traditions, and its way of solving problems. In our case, it involves a lot of laughter, a bit of chaos, and an unending supply of love. Whether you're a detective in training or just here for the dessert, you're in for a treat. Let's dive into the mystery of the missing churros and discover that, sometimes, the simplest ingredients make for the most memorable stories.

Table of Contents

1. **Prologue**
   - Welcome to Another Luera Family Adventure
2. **Preface**
   - The Essence of Family Tales and Churro Capers
3. **Chapter 1: The Festive Fiasco**
   - Birthday Preparations and the Great Churro Heist
4. **Chapter 2: The Churro Chase**
   - Accusations and Investigations Begin
5. **Chapter 3: Twin Detectives on the Trail**
   - Kawika and Keoni Take the Lead
6. **Chapter 4: The Sweet Culprit**
   - El Padre's Blissful Indulgence Revealed
7. **Chapter 5: Sugary Solutions and Surprises**
   - Granita's Hidden Stash Saves the Day
8. **Epilogue: Laughter and Lessons Learned**
   - Reflecting on the Day's Memorable Events
9. **Character Descriptions**
   - Meet the Luera Family Characters
10. **Sneak Peek: "Is La Llorona for Real?"**
    - Preview of the Next Family Mystery

Chapter 1: The Festive Fiasco

It was a sunny afternoon at El Padre's house, and the entire place was buzzing with excitement and the aroma of fresh churros. Today was Granita's 55th birthday, and her daughters, Bianca, Vivian, and Lyla, had been planning this blowout for months. The house was transformed into a vibrant replica of Granita's father's hometown village in Mexico, complete with colorful papel picado fluttering in the breeze.

Amidst the laughter and mariachi music, the twin tornadoes, Kawika and Keoni, raced around the bath tub-sized copper pot filled with Carnitas. These six-year-old bundles of energy, known for their nonstop "full throttle" mode, were already plotting their next mischievous adventure, much to the amusement and slight concern of their older sister, Noa.

As the mariachi band played their final notes, El Padre gathered Lizzy, Mila, Royalty, Romona, and Noa to help with a very special task—carrying the tray of meticulously tested and perfected churros out to the patio for G-Ma's birthday song. However, as they approached the dining room, a collective gasp echoed through the air. The tray was empty!

Chapter 2: The Churro Chase

"All the churros are missing!" screamed the cousins in unison, their voices filled with shock and a hint of despair. Panic ensued as they darted out to the patio, announcing the great churro disappearance to the gathered family and guests.

Accusations flew like the piñata bat earlier that day. Could Noa, known for her sleepwalking, have taken a nocturnal snack trip? Or perhaps Lizzy, whose love for churros was unmatched? The family's initial amusement soon turned into a genuine mystery, prompting an emergency family meeting beside the garden fountain.

Granita called for order. "Let's not jump to conclusions. We'll get to the bottom of this, one churro crumb at a time," she declared, much to the relief of the worried party planners.

Determined to salvage the party and their grandmother's spirits, the cousins formed an impromptu detective squad, with Kawika and Keoni leading the charge. The twins, notorious for their relentless energy, were now on a mission fueled by the dual thrill of mystery and the promise of churros.

Chapter 3: Twin Detectives on the Trail

With iPad in hand, Kawika and Keoni turned their boundless energy into investigative prowess. They darted from guest to guest, gathering clues and alibis, their youthful exuberance causing both amusement and mild annoyance. Their investigation took them from the shadowy corners of the backyard to the bustling kitchen, where they interrogated the caterers with a seriousness that belied their years.

Their breakthrough came when they decided to review footage from the iPad, which they had serendipitously left recording in the dining room. The video revealed a surprising yet familiar figure engaged in the act of churro consumption.

Chapter 4: The Sweet Culprit

As the curious and excited crowd of family members huddled around the flickering iPad screen, the twins, Kawika and Keoni, beamed with pride at their successful sleuthing. Amidst the colorful backdrop of the party, the video played, revealing El Padre in a rare, unguarded moment of indulgence. There he was, sneaking into the dining room under the guise of checking on the decorations, only to succumb to the temptation of the perfectly fried churros. Each bite was taken with a look of blissful guilt, his eyes almost closing in delight, savoring the sugary sweetness that Bianca had so masterfully prepared.

Vivian said, "Dad, your eyes rolled to the back of your head like a great white shark!" Lyla turned to the cousins and said, "It was a work of art; my dad deserves an Oscar for his performance!"

The room erupted in a mix of laughter and playful jeers. El Padre, with sugar still dusting his mustache, gave a sheepish shrug and chuckled, "They were just too good to resist!" His jovial confession, far from causing upset, sparked a round of affectionate ribbing. Noa playfully scolded him, "And you always tell us to save some for everyone!" El Padre, with a twinkle in his eye, retorted, "Mija, the spirit was willing, but the flesh was weak—and the churros were too tempting!"

This light-hearted moment exemplified the family's loving nature, turning what could have been a scolding into a moment of shared humor and warmth. It was these moments that truly defined the Lueras—always ready to find joy and laughter, even in mishaps.

Chapter 5: Sugary Solutions and Surprises

Not to be outdone by the drama, Granita, ever the matriarch and sage of the family, stood up, her eyes crinkling with mirth. "Well, it seems we might have lost one battle with the churros, but the war isn't over yet!" With a flourish typical of her dramatic flair, she revealed her secret stash: an even larger tray of churros, hidden behind a decorative panel in the living room. "A good hostess always prepares for emergencies," she declared, her voice full of pride and a hint of I-told-you-so.

The family cheered as the hidden churros made their grand entrance. The party, briefly subdued by the mystery, now returned to its full, vibrant life. Children and adults alike lined up, their plates ready for the sugary treat that had been the day's unexpected star. As they bit into the warm, crispy churros, the earlier tensions melted away, replaced by the sweet taste of Bianca's perfect recipe and Granita's foresight.

This sweet turn of events was a testament to Granita's wisdom and her understanding of the family's dynamics. Her ability to anticipate and her readiness with a backup plan not only saved the celebration but also elevated her status even further in the eyes of her family.

CHAPTER 1.

Epilogue: Laughter and Lessons Learned

As the evening stars began to twinkle in the twilight sky, the Luera family sat back, full of churros and contentment. The day had been one of surprises and revelations, but most of all, it had been a day of unity and laughter. The churro caper, which had started as a source of mystery and slight consternation, had evolved into a cherished new memory, woven into the family's rich tapestry of stories.

As El Padre helped Granita blow out her candles, surrounded by the smiling faces of their family, the true lesson of the day shone clearly: in the Luera family, no mystery was too small to bring everyone together, and no mistake was too big to forgive. It was these moments—filled with laughter, love, and a bit of detective work—that kept the family bonds strong and the stories even richer.

Tonight, as they cleaned up the last of the party and put away the trays and decorations, each member of the Luera family knew they had added another great story to their collection. They were stories that would be retold and laughed about at many future gatherings, reminders of the day they all came together over the mystery of the missing churros.

Character Descriptions

El Padre (David Luera): The jovial and mischievous patriarch of the Luera family. Known for his love of snacks and an endless supply of entertaining stories, El Padre is often the center of family fun and occasional inadvertent mischief.

Granita (Gabby Luera): The wise and loving matriarch of the family. G-Ma is revered for her baking skills, particularly her churros, and her ability to anticipate the needs of her family. She's the keeper of traditions and the resolver of crises with her hidden stashes and backup plans.

Lizzy: A sharp-witted and resourceful cousin with a particular fondness for churros. Liz is known for her quick thinking and often takes a leadership role in the cousins' adventures.

Mila: The artistic cousin with a vibrant imagination. Mila is often found with a sketchbook in hand, ready to capture the family's antics or conjure up elaborate theories about the smallest mysteries.

Royalty: Bold and spirited, Royalty is the natural leader among the cousins. Her charismatic personality and daring nature often propel the group into new adventures.

Romona: The storyteller of the group, Romana has a flair for drama and a talent for making every family tale sound epic. Her vivid recounting adds depth and excitement to their exploits.

Noa: The logical thinker and sometimes the voice of reason among her more impulsive cousins. Noa's analytical mind is crucial in solving the mysteries that the Luera family often encounters.

Kawika and Keoni: The energetic twin brothers of Noa, known for their "full throttle" approach to life. At six years old, they are curious, adventurous, and a handful in the best possible way. Their boundless energy and nascent detective skills make them central figures in the family's escapades.

Bianca, Vivian, and Lyla: Granita's daughters and the meticulous planners behind the family gatherings. Each brings her own set of skills to the events, from Bianca's culinary prowess to Vivian's organizational abilities and Lyla's decorative talents.

These characters form the heart of the Luera family, each adding their unique flavor to the family's rich tapestry of stories and adventures.

Sneak Peek: "Is La Llorona for Real?"

As autumn leaves begin to paint the ground with fiery hues, the Luera family is gearing up for an adventure that promises more chills than the crisp night air. In the next chapter of their lively family saga, they venture into the dense woods for a weekend camping trip that coincides with the eerie whispers of Halloween.

Gathered around a crackling campfire, the scene is set under a crescent moon that casts a silvery glow on the eager faces of the Luera cousins. As marshmallows roast and hot cocoa warms their hands, El Padre decides it's the perfect moment to delve into the chilling tale of La Llorona—the weeping woman whose mournful cries are said to haunt the riverbanks, searching for her lost children.

The story begins as all good ghost tales do, with wide eyes and hushed voices. El Padre, a masterful storyteller, recounts the legend with a flair that sends shivers through the listeners. He speaks of a beautiful woman betrayed by love, doomed to wander the Earth for eternity. As the tale unfolds, the wind seems to carry a sorrowful wail, turning the children's tentative giggles into nervous glances towards the shadowy trees.

Curiosity, as it often does with the Lueras, quickly overcomes fear. The cousins, led by the daring Royalty and the skeptical Noa, hatch a plan to investigate the mysterious sounds. Armed with flashlights, a camera, and an unquenchable thirst for the truth, they set out towards the river, the supposed haunt of the spectral weeper.

Their journey through the woods is filled with the natural sounds of the night, each rustle and crack fueling their imagination. Every shadow hints at movement; every breeze carries a note of despair. The line between story and reality blurs as the adventure deepens, turning their quest into a thrilling exploration of the unknown.

Are the cries they hear carried on the wind merely the calls of a night bird, or is there truth to the legend? Each step brings them closer to an answer, weaving their own experiences with the threads of the tale they've been told. This camping trip, intended as a simple escape to nature, transforms into an unforgettable encounter with folklore and family bravery.

In "Is La Llorona for Real?" join the Luera cousins as they navigate the mysterious and often eerie landscape of legend and reality. Dive into this ghostly adventure where fears are faced, legends are explored, and the bond of family proves to be the strongest guide through the shadows of the unknown. As the night unfolds, they will discover that some stories—whether mere myths or startling truths—have the power to bring them together in ways they never imagined.

Made in the USA
Columbia, SC
16 December 2024